RAPUNZEL

A Favorite Story in Rhythm and Rhyme

Retold by JONATHAN PEALE

Illustrated by VILLIE KARABATZIA

Music Arranged and Produced by STEVEN C MUSIC

CANTATA
LEARNING

WWW.CANTATALEARNING.COM

CANTATA LEARNING

Published by Cantata Learning
1710 Roe Crest Drive
North Mankato, MN 56003
www.cantatalearning.com

A note to educators and librarians from the publisher: Cantata Learning has provided the following data to assist in book processing and suggested use of Cantata Learning product.

Publisher's Cataloging-in-Publication Data
Prepared by Librarian Consultant: Ann-Marie Begnaud
Library of Congress Control Number: 2015958221
    Rapunzel : A Favorite Story in Rhythm and Rhyme
    Series: Fairy Tale Tunes
    Retold by Jonathan Peale
    Illustrated by Villie Karabatzia
    Summary: The fairy tale of Rapunzel comes to life with music and full-color illustrations.
    ISBN: 978-1-63290-618-2 (library binding/CD)
    ISBN: 978-1-63290-640-3 (paperback/CD)
Suggested Dewey and Subject Headings:
    Dewey: E 398.2
    LCSH Subject Headings: Fairy tales – Juvenile literature. | Fairy tales – Songs and music – Texts. | Fairy tales – Juvenile sound recordings.
    Sears Subject Headings: Fairy tales. | Princesses. | School songbooks. | Children's songs. | Popular music.
    BISAC Subject Headings: JUVENILE FICTION / Fairy Tales & Folklore / Adaptations. | JUVENILE FICTION / Stories in Verse. | JUVENILE FICTION / Royalty.

Book design and art direction, Tim Palin Creative
Editorial direction, Flat Sole Studio
Music direction, Elizabeth Draper
Music arranged and produced by Steven C Music

Printed in the United States of America in North Mankato, Minnesota.
072016   0335CGF16

ACCESS THE MUSIC!

SCAN CODE WITH MOBILE APP

CANTATALEARNING.COM

The story of "Rapunzel" is an old German fairy tale about a princess. A witch locked Rapunzel in a tall **tower** in the woods. The tower didn't have any stairs, so the witch used Rapunzel's long golden hair as a ladder to climb into the tower.

To find out what happens when a prince sees Rapunzel up in her tower, turn the page and sing along!

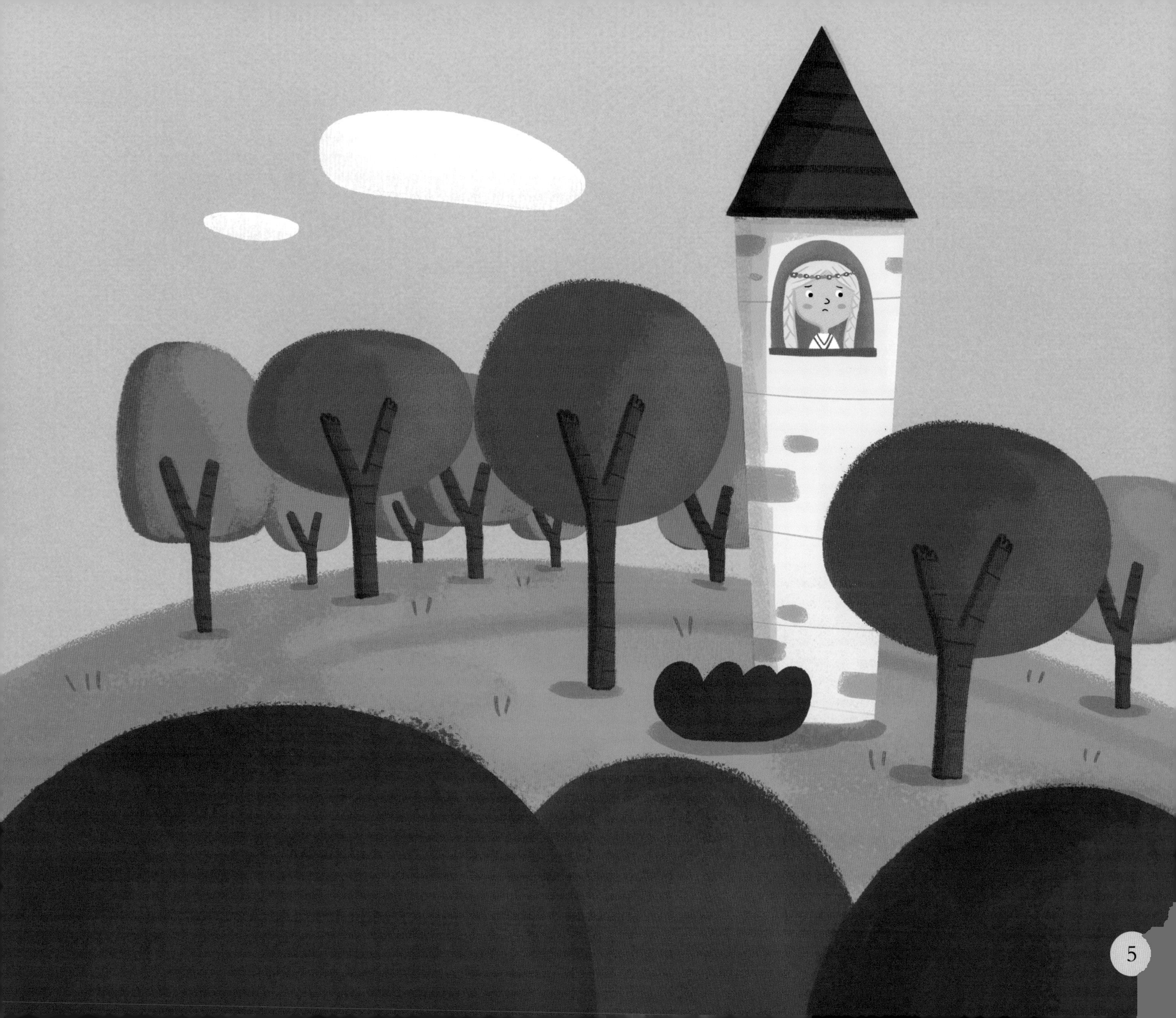

A prince was riding through the woods.
He saw something that was not good.

A tower stood very tall,
without a way up at all.

The prince saw a scary witch below,
staring up at a high window.

There, a princess looked out,
and the witch began to shout.

Rapunzel, Rapunzel,
let down your hair
that I may climb
the golden stair!

Rapunzel, Rapunzel,
with hair so long,
listen to the call of my song.

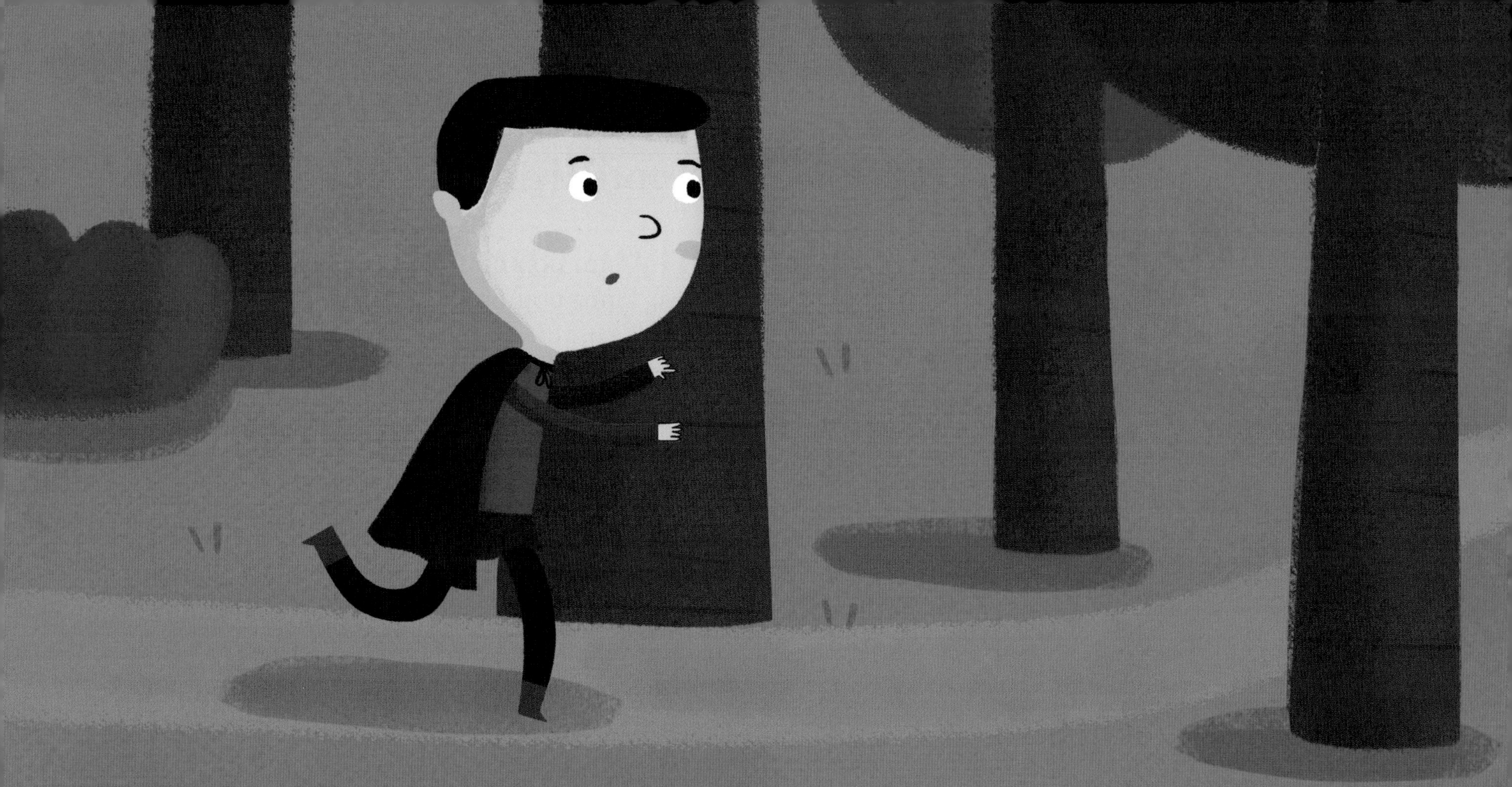

Rapunzel let down her hair, just so.
The witch climbed up to that high window.

The prince watched without a sound,
and after a while, the witch climbed down.

The prince's head was all **awhirl**.
He wanted to meet that beautiful girl!

So he ran to the foot of the tower tall,
and from his mouth came a hopeful call.

Rapunzel, Rapunzel,
let down your hair
that I may climb the golden stair!

Rapunzel, Rapunzel,
with hair so long,
listen to the call of my song.

The prince and Rapunzel fell in love,
in that tower high above.

But just as he was about to go,
the witch appeared in the window.

The witch pushed the prince out, another surprise!
He fell on bushes that scratched out his eyes.

The witch cut off Rapunzel's hair
and sent her far away from there.

So Rapunzel **wandered**, far away,
for many a year and many a day.

She wandered morning, noon, and night,
until she saw a **familiar** sight!

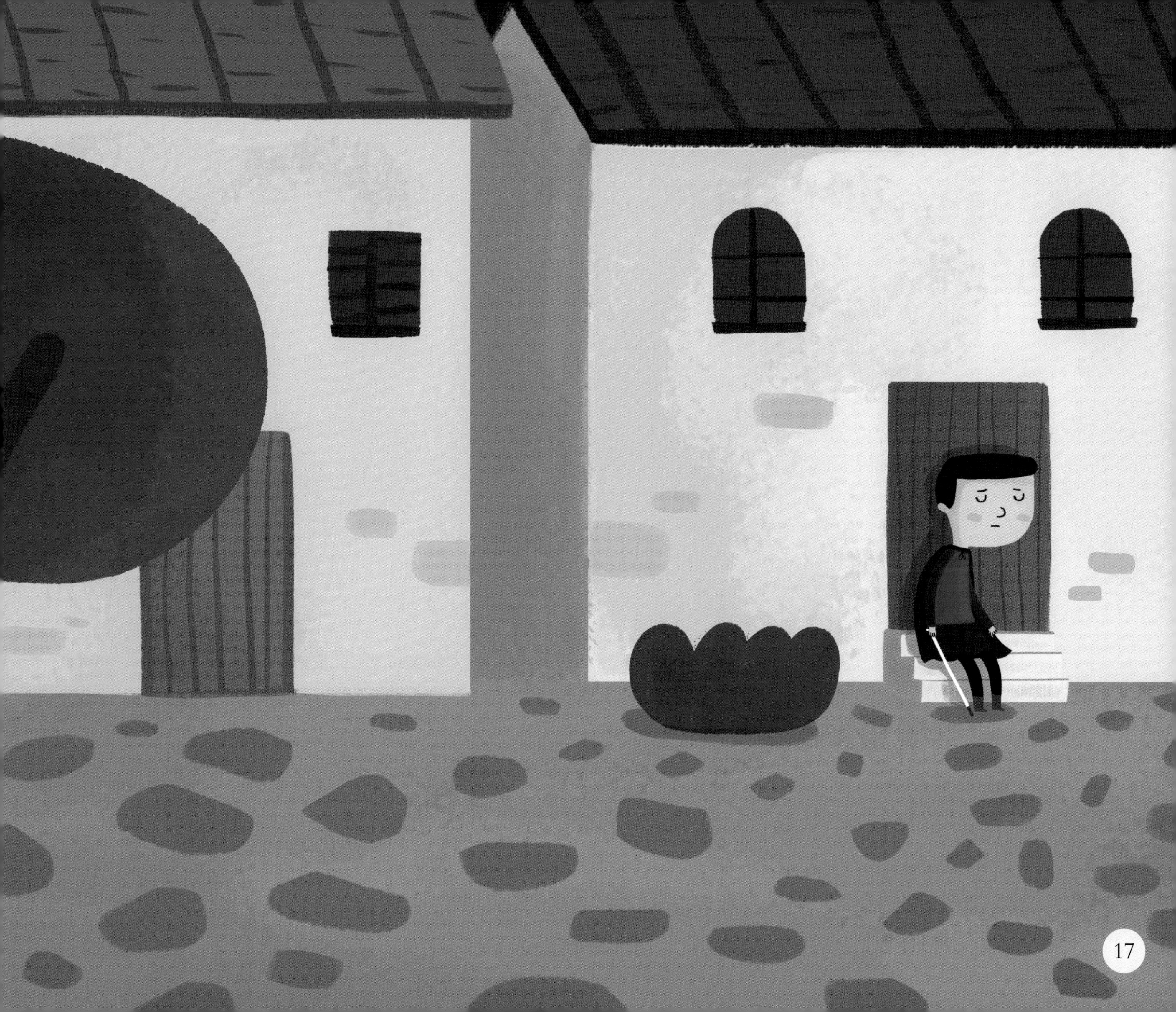

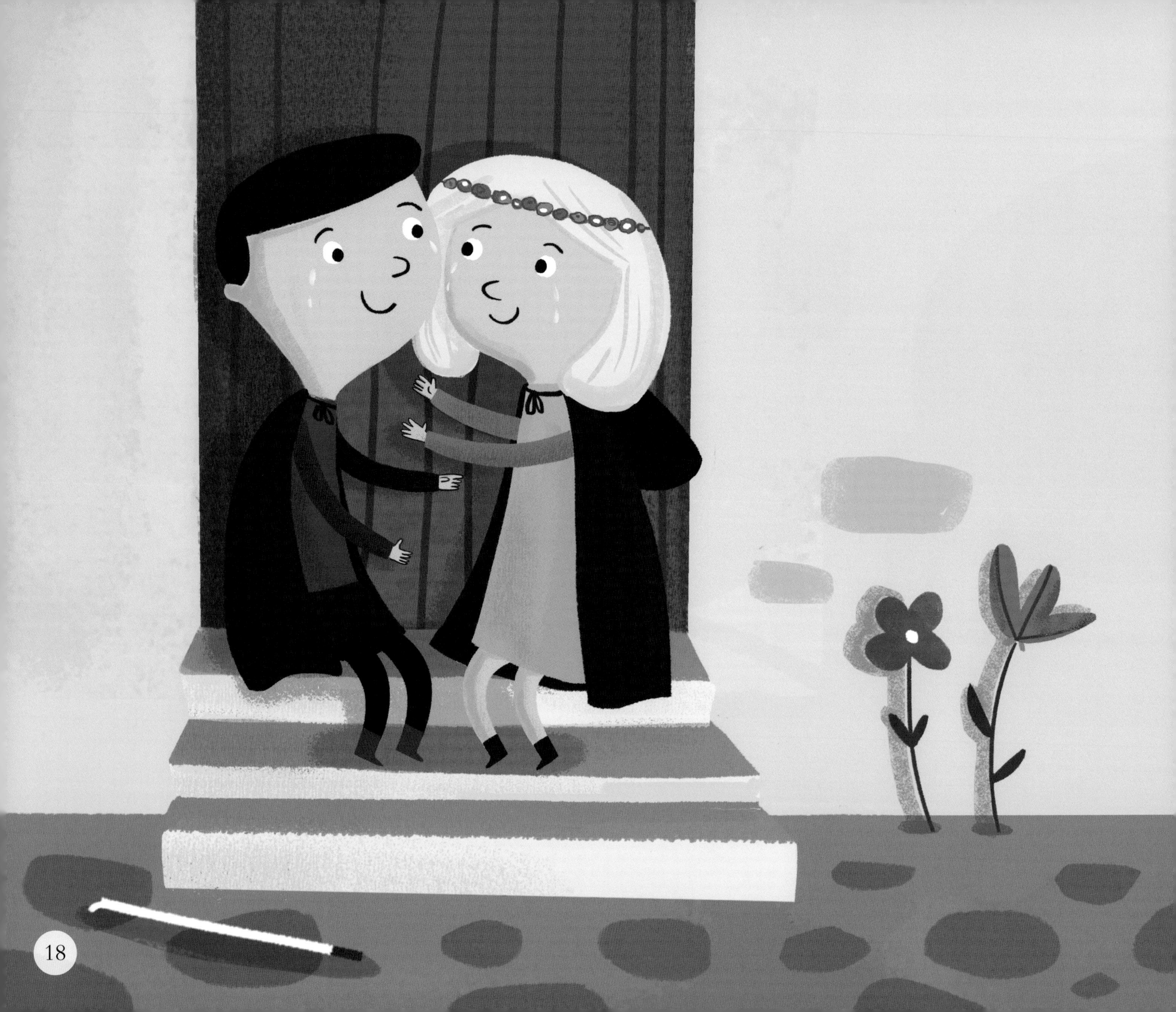

She found the prince and heard his **cane** tap!
Rapunzel went and laid his head in her lap.

As her tears touched the prince's eyes,
he could see again, and the prince cried.

Rapunzel, Rapunzel,
let down your hair
that I may climb the golden stair!

Rapunzel, Rapunzel,
with hair so long,
listen to the call of my song.

SONG LYRICS
Rapunzel

A prince was riding through the woods.
He saw something that was not good.
A tower stood very tall,
without a way up at all.

The prince saw a scary witch below,
staring up at a high window.
There, a princess looked out,
and the witch began to shout.

Rapunzel, Rapunzel,
let down your hair
that I may climb the golden stair!

Rapunzel, Rapunzel,
with hair so long,
listen to the call of my song.

Rapunzel let down her hair, just so.
The witch climbed up to that high window.
The prince watched without a sound,
and after a while, the witch climbed down.

The prince's head was all awhirl.
He wanted to meet that beautiful girl!
So he ran to the foot of the tower tall,
and from his mouth came a hopeful call.

Rapunzel, Rapunzel,
let down your hair
that I may climb the golden stair!

Rapunzel, Rapunzel,
with hair so long,
listen to the call of my song.

The prince and Rapunzel fell in love,
in that tower high above.
But just as he was about to go,
the witch appeared in the window.

The witch pushed the prince out, another surprise!
He fell on bushes that scratched out his eyes.
The witch cut off Rapunzel's hair
and sent her far away from there.

So Rapunzel wandered, far away,
for many a year and many a day.
She wandered morning, noon, and night,
until she saw a familiar sight!

She found the prince and heard his cane tap!
Rapunzel went and laid his head in her lap.
As her tears touched the prince's eyes,
he could see again, and the prince cried.

Rapunzel, Rapunzel,
let down your hair
that I may climb the golden stair!

Rapunzel, Rapunzel,
with hair so long,
listen to the call of my song.

GLOSSARY

awhirl—feeling like something is spinning

cane—a curved stick that provides support as a person walks

familiar—something that is well known to someone

tower—a tall structure

wandered—moved about without a particular purpose or place to go

GUIDED READING ACTIVITIES

1. The witch kept Rapunzel in the tower so she couldn't have any other friends. Have you ever wanted to keep something just for yourself? What was it?

2. If you could grow your hair as long as Rapunzel's, would you? Why or why not?

3. If you had to live in a tower, what things would you bring with you? Draw a picture of your perfect tower home.

TO LEARN MORE

Gorman, Karyn. *Rapunzel and the Prince of Pop*. New York: Crabtree Publishing Company, 2015.

Guillain, Charlotte. *Ratpunzel*. Chicago: Raintree, 2014.

Gunderson, Jessica. *Really, Rapunzel Needed a Haircut! The Story of Rapunzel, as Told by Dame Gothel*. North Mankato, MN: Picture Window Books, a Capstone imprint, 2014.

Meister, Cari. *Rapunzel: 3 Beloved Tales*. North Mankato, MN: Picture Window Books, a Capstone imprint, 2015.